# QUERZOL
# THE SWAMP MONSTER

## BY ADAM BLADE

ORCHARD

With special thanks to Tabitha Jones

*For Reggie Loveridge*

www.beastquest.co.uk

ORCHARD BOOKS

First published in Great Britain in 2019 by The Watts Publishing Group

1 3 5 7 9 10 8 6 4 2

Text © 2019 Beast Quest Limited.
Cover and inside illustrations by Steve Sims
© Beast Quest Limited 2019

Beast Quest is a registered trademark of Beast Quest Limited
Series created by Beast Quest Limited, London

A CIP catalogue record for this book is available from the British Library.

ISBN 978 1 40834 344 9

Printed in Great Britain

The paper and board used in this book are made from wood from responsible sources

Orchard Books
An imprint of Hachette Children's Group
Part of The Watts Publishing Group Limited
Carmelite House, 50 Victoria Embankment, London EC4Y 0DZ

An Hachette UK Company
www.hachette.co.uk
www.hachettechildrens.co.uk

# Welcome to the world of Beast Quest!

Tom was once an ordinary village boy, until he travelled to the City, met King Hugo and discovered his destiny. Now he is the Master of the Beasts, sworn to defend Avantia and its people against Evil. Tom draws on the might of the magical Golden Armour, and is protected by powerful tokens granted to him by the Good Beasts of Avantia. Tom and his loyal companion Elenna are always ready to visit new lands and tackle the enemies of the realm.

While there's blood in his veins, Tom will never give up the Quest…

THE WILDLANDS

MANGROVE
SWAMP

TO
AVANTIA ↘

There are special gold coins to collect in this book. You will earn one coin for every chapter you read.

Find out what to do with your coins at the end of the book.

# CONTENTS

It's been many years since I crossed the borders of Avantia. I can't say I've missed the place much. Last time I was here, my plan to conquer the kingdom was foiled by a mere boy, though he calls himself their Master of the Beasts.

Now I serve a new and cruel master. Though he looks like a man, he has the cold heart of a monster. We have travelled day and night from the Wildlands north of Avantia's frozen wastes, and at last the walls of the City loom into view.

I have heard the boy Tom is still alive. I wonder what he will think when he sees me again. And I wonder if he will understand the terrible danger that is about to be unleashed.

One thing is certain – the kingdom and its people are going to suffer a terrible fate.

Yours,

Kapra the Witch

# THE QUEEN'S
# BIRTHDAY

A full moon hung low in the evening
sky, and the scent of roasting meat
wafted from the palace kitchens.
Music filled the courtyard and
dancing couples flitted past Tom as
he pushed his dinner plate away. "I
can't eat another bite," he sighed,
turning to Elenna, who sat beside

him at the banqueting table.

His friend put down the chicken leg she'd been nibbling. "I guess that means two slices of Aroha's birthday cake for me, then," she said, smiling.

Tom glanced up the table that ran the length of the courtyard, to where King Hugo and Queen Aroha sat on a raised dais. The jewels in the king's crown glinted as he nodded in time with the music. Beside him, the queen beamed as she watched the dancing couples. Nearby sat an enormous cake, baked in the shape of the queen's palace in Tangala, in honour of her birthday. Despite his full stomach, Tom's mouth watered.

"Don't even think of taking my

slice!" he said, turning back to
Elenna. She was gazing across the
courtyard, pointing at something.

"Look!" she laughed. "I
never thought I'd see Daltec
dancing!" The young wizard

whirled past, hand in hand with one of the queen's maids. But, as they watched, Daltec stepped on the hem of his long robe and stumbled. The maid caught Daltec's arm and steadied him, and the pair set off again, blushing and laughing.

Elenna winced. "Well, sort of dancing anyway..."

The ding of metal on glass cut through the festivities. Tom peered across the crowded courtyard to see a small man in a feathered hat and a deep-blue velvet robe, holding a glass and knife aloft.

*A bard*, Tom realised, leaning forward with excitement. The musician set the utensils down, and picked up his lute. His eyes glinted as an expectant hush filled the square.

"Ladies and gentlemen!" the slight man called in a strong, rich voice. "Please take your seats. His Majesty King Hugo has requested a very special song." The bard paused to strum a note. "A song of tragic bravery and heroism. It is the story of Prince Angelo and his courageous deeds in the Border Wars, more than thirty years ago." The courtyard quickly cleared as the guests returned to their benches and the band retired, leaving only the bard, alone in the centre. The man's dark eyes ran the length of the table and he smiled, strumming a low chord, and began to sing.

Tom knew the tune well, and settled back as the bard's rich voice conjured scenes from long ago. The song told the tale of King Hugo's elder brother, a brave and valiant young man. It sang of how their father, the old King Theo, had given his heir a priceless golden ring before the prince rode away to defend Avantia's northern borders against an invasion of barbarians from the Wildlands. The bard's deep voice filled the night as he sang of Angelo's legendary swordsmanship, and the mighty power of his right arm. How Angelo and his troops fought a long battle, thwarting many attacks...but the enemy was too great…

The bard's voice fell to a hush, the tone of the song changing. Tom glanced up to see the guests still

and silent. King Hugo lifted a hand to wipe his gleaming eyes, and Tom felt a lump form in his own throat. Solemn now, the bard sang on, telling of how even Angelo's matchless strength and skill couldn't save him from the northern barbarians.

"*Never to return...*" the bard sang finally, his head hung low, and his eyes brimmed with sorrow as the last chord echoed to silence. For a moment everyone sat still, until Hugo cleared his throat and began to applaud. Tom and Elenna joined in, and before long, the whole courtyard rang with cheers. Tom smiled at the happy, torchlit faces, feeling the song's melancholy spell lifting. But when he looked up towards Captain Harkman – who was atop the courtyard's wall, keeping watch – a cold finger traced his spine. Harkman had been standing at ease for most of the night, but now he leaned out over the parapet, his body stiff and tense. *He's seen something...*

Tom put a hand on Elenna's shoulder. "I'll be back in a moment," he said, pointing up towards the captain. Then he slipped from his seat and skirted around the courtyard wall, until he reached the winding stair to the battlements. He climbed up to the high stone walkway. The dark city spread out before him, scattered with the flickering lights of torches. Harkman turned. At the sight of the old captain's drawn and stern expression, Tom's worry deepened.

"What's wrong?" he asked.

Harkman pointed to the shadowy fields beyond the city's wall. "A party of riders, approaching fast," he said.

Tom called on the enhanced eyesight of his golden helmet – which was part of his magical

armour, kept safe in the palace vault – to look out, feeling his chest tighten with dread. At least fifty armoured men on horseback were approaching the city gate. "They're armed," Tom told the captain, "but I can't see an Avantian flag."

"No," Harkman said. "There's no squad or detachment on deployment right now – not in this kingdom, nor any other. These men aren't Avantian soldiers." The captain took a horn from his belt and sent out three short notes. The music and laughter in the square died away, replaced by hushed, anxious voices. "Secure the gate!" Harkman bellowed. The cry was taken up by a sentry hidden in the shadows below, and passed on by the next sentry and then the next, the command echoing out across the city. Down in the courtyard, the guests began to flee.

"Get word to the king," Captain Harkman told Tom, "then meet me at the city gates." Tom nodded, and followed the captain down from the wall.

Before long, Tom and Elenna were hurrying through the darkened city, weapons drawn. King Hugo and Daltec kept pace behind them. They reached the barred city gate and clambered breathlessly up the gatehouse steps to find Harkman at the parapet, staring at the group of men below. Poised at intervals along the length of the wall, archers held their bows ready. Tom's skin tingled with the tension thrumming in the cool night air.

A single rider broke from the group and rode slowly forward, sword drawn.

"Prepare to fire," Harkman called to his men. Tom heard the creak of bows pulled taut.

The rider stopped close enough to the gate for Tom to make out dents and scores in his battle-worn armour. Then he lifted his hand and drew off his helmet in a single movement. With a tingle of surprise, Tom felt like he recognised the stern features and dark eyes gazing up at them.

For a long moment, no one moved. Then, suddenly, Hugo let out a strange, broken cry. Tom turned to see the king clutching his chest, his face pale in the half-darkness and his eyes wide and shocked. "It can't be…" Hugo whispered, then he raised his voice: "Hold fire! Put down your bows!"

As Harkman turned a questioning look to the king, Hugo pointed with a quivering finger. "That's no enemy," he gasped. "That's my brother, Angelo!"

# ANGELO'S TALE

With a rattling *clank*, the palace gates swung open. Tom and Elenna followed King Hugo and Captain Harkman from the battlements, down the dusky stairwell into the courtyard.

*For more than thirty years*, he thought, *everyone believed Angelo was dead! Where can he have been all this time?*

Nerves tingling, Tom waited with
Elenna, King Hugo and Captain
Harkman as Angelo rode through the
gate, his deep-set eyes glinting in his
stern, hawk-like face. His soldiers
followed close behind, each one
broad and powerfully built, sitting
tall in the saddle. All of them wore
full armour, except the last – a slight
figure, cloaked and hooded, their
features hidden in shadow. Angelo
swung from his horse and strode
towards the king. The cloaked figure
dismounted too, hurrying to Angelo's
side and throwing back the hood.
The breath caught in Tom's throat
as he recognised the woman's sharp

features and long, grey hair.

*Kapra!*

"What's that witch doing here?"
Elenna whispered. "She's supposed
to be behind bars!"

Tom clenched his teeth, fighting the reflex to reach for his sword. While he now often fought alongside Kapra's daughter, Petra, he had hoped he would never see Kapra again. The evil witch had once tried to summon Raksha the Mirror Demon to do her bidding. She had eventually been arrested by Kerlo, the Gorgonian gatekeeper, but only after throwing Avantia into great peril.

*Why would the king's brother bring a villainous witch to the palace?*

But King Hugo didn't seem to have noticed Kapra at all. As Angelo stepped towards him, Hugo sank to his knees, shaking with emotion.

"Greetings, little brother," Angelo said, offering Hugo a hand. Hugo stood and drew Angelo into a hearty embrace.

After a long moment, the king stepped back, searching Angelo's face, his eyes full of wonder. "Angelo, I…" he stuttered. "We thought you dead. Where have you been for so many years?"

"It is a long story," Angelo said. "And one I would prefer to tell inside the walls of my old home."

"Of course!" Hugo said. "Forgive me. We will see to your horses, and find food and drink for your men. Follow me."

Tom's spine tingled with a strange

mixture of anticipation and dread as he and Elenna paced after the king and his brother.

*This should be a story worth hearing...*

Torches threw flickering shadows over the throne room walls as Tom and Elenna took their seats near the fire. Daltec and Captain Harkman shared a bench, while Angelo sat alone, gazing into the flames. King Hugo sat opposite his brother, studying his face keenly, as if Angelo might vanish. Now that Angelo had removed his armour, Tom could see that he was both taller and broader than the king, though leaner, with a hollow look to his cheeks. He was darker, too, his eyes almost black and his long hair streaked with grey.

"As you can see, I was not killed in battle," Angelo said, finally lifting his eyes from the flames, "though in many ways, it might have been a kinder fate. For the last thirty years, my men and I have lived and fought in the Wildlands, defending the kingdom's borders from the northern barbarians and their four Beasts."

Elenna shot Tom a puzzled frown, and Tom knew what she was thinking. He was thinking the same thing. *Four Beasts so close to our borders, and I was unaware?*

"The battle has been relentless," Angelo went on, his voice rough with fatigue. "We almost believed it would never end. I defeated one of the barbarians' Beasts myself, though not before many brave soldiers were lost to its claws. But now, after almost three decades of raids and skirmishes, the war is finally over. The enemy is defeated, and I can return home, knowing Avantia is safe."

King Hugo shook his head, his eyes filled with awe. "Truly, yours must be the greatest sacrifice any Avantian warrior has made," he said. "Our father would have been proud…" Hugo trailed off, a choke in his voice, then cleared his throat. "Tell me, how did you finally defeat our enemy?"

"Only with the help of Kapra," Angelo said. "Her healing magic allowed me to survive a terrible wound, suffered at the blade of the barbarian leader." Angelo, sitting upright now, met each of their eyes in turn, then drew back the loose collar of his tunic. Tom winced at the sight of a deep, angry scar puckering the flesh of Angelo's chest, right above his heart. "Once I had recovered, my troops and I were able to turn back the tide, and, with the Good Witch's magic, break through enemy lines."

Captain Harkman snorted. "That's the first time I've heard Kapra called a 'Good Witch'," he said. "I'm sure she had her own reasons for helping you, as we'll find out soon enough."

Tom nodded. *Just what I was thinking...*

But Angelo turned sharply on the captain, his eyes narrowed and his chin held high. "Well, you needn't worry," he said. "She won't be using her magic to clean the soldiers' boots, so your job is quite safe."

Harkman's face flushed as red as if he'd been slapped, and Tom felt his own face grow warm. *Why would Angelo say something so cruel?* The captain opened his mouth as if to

respond, but King Hugo lifted a hand.

"Brother, Captain Harkman has become a fine warrior and the leader of my army since you last saw him as a younger man. He is a loyal friend."

Angelo scowled. "Yet he speaks ill of the woman who saved my life!"

Tom couldn't remain quiet any longer. "Your Highness, it's reasonable that Harkman should worry Kapra might mean us ill," he said. "She has used her magic against Avantia before."

Angelo turned to glare at Tom, his lip curled in disgust. "Insubordinate! Just like your father!" Tom felt a stab of outrage which must have shown in his face, for Angelo went on. "Oh, yes – the unfortunate resemblance is clear. I will not hear another word against Kapra from you or that fool of a boot boy. In fact, for her service, the Good Witch will be officially pardoned by the king of Avantia."

Tom turned to see King Hugo shaking his head, frowning.

But Angelo went on, louder than before: "The *rightful* king," he said, turning his dark eyes on Hugo. "You have looked after the kingdom while I was away, little brother. But now it is time for me to claim the crown that is my birthright." Tom felt his stomach drop away. Daltec and Elenna both gasped. But, with barely a pause, King Hugo bowed and took off his golden crown, handing it to Angelo.

With a wolflike grin, Angelo placed it on his greying hair. Then he turned

to Captain Harkman. "Now you will
clean my boots," he said.

Captain Harkman flushed red,
then went pale. He looked to Hugo,
but the former king shook his head
gently.

"Now, young Tristan!" Angelo snapped, speaking the captain's name as if it was an insult.

Harkman's hands shook with suppressed fury as he kneeled at the new king's feet. Then, with the sleeve of his tunic, he started to buff the muddy leather.

A cold, hollow feeling settled in Tom's gut as he watched. *How can this be happening?* he thought. *Is this some kind of bad dream?*

# THE GREEDY KING

Clangs and shouts broke into Tom's
uneasy dreams, jolting him awake.
His head throbbed from tossing
and turning all night, but he shook
away the pain and leaped out of bed.
In half-darkness, he crossed to the
window to peer out. Below, mounted
soldiers filled the courtyard and
horses dragged heavily loaded carts.

*What's going on?*

Tom pulled on his tunic and boots, buckled on his sword, and hurried from his chamber to investigate. He reached the courtyard at the same moment as Daltec and Aduro. Their faces wore worried frowns.

Captain Harkman stood by one of the carts, speaking in a low, angry rumble to Kapra: "There's no need! The kingdom is at peace!"

"The people must know they have a new king," Kapra said, "and that he is a strong and capable ruler."

"Then send a messenger, or hold a feast," Harkman said, "don't send warriors. And what are all those empty chests for?" He pointed to the carts. Tom saw heavy, metal-bound wooden chests stacked in the back.

A huge, weather-beaten soldier turned from overseeing the loading of the carts and strode towards them. Pale blond hair hung loose to his shoulders, and impatience smouldered in his almost colourless blue eyes. "The chests are for the new royal tax," he snapped, his accent one Tom had never heard before. *Is he a wild man from the north who changed sides?* Tom wondered. *If so, he's the first I've ever heard of doing that.*

"But the royal tax has already been collected," Harkman said. "We can't ask people to give even more."

"The king needs more," Kapra said, "to fund enhancements to his military. It will reassure the people they are well protected."

"Ridiculous!" Harkman cried. "My men have never needed to steal from the people to do their jobs. My men and I will have no part of this!"

Kapra's lips spread into a spiteful smile. "His Majesty anticipated you might defy his orders – that's why he's given me the authority to strip you of your rank." The witch pointed at the captain. Blue light crackled from her fingertips and lashed towards him.

Tom and Elenna exchanged a look of alarm as Harkman let out an angry yelp. When the light faded, his wrists were trapped in iron manacles.

"Take him into custody!" Kapra said, turning to the blond soldier.

"You can't," Daltec cried, stepping forward, but Aduro pulled him

back, gesturing towards the palace doors with a tilt of the head. Tom looked over to see Angelo, dressed in a jewelled purple robe, striding through.

"What's going on?" he bellowed.

*This must be a mistake!* Tom thought. *Surely if I explain...* "Your Majesty," he said, "Kapra was just telling the captain about a new tax. Harkman was trying to explain that such a tax would be an unfair burden on the people of Avantia."

But even as he spoke, Tom could see Angelo's face colouring, his jaw tightening. "How dare you?" the new king bellowed, his voice quivering with fury. Tom felt a tingle of relief – Kapra was going to get a dressing-down from the king. Then he realised Angelo was not shouting at the witch. He was looking right at Tom. "How dare you question my orders!" He turned to the pale blond soldier, who was now lounging against a cart. "I think this whelp needs to be taught a lesson, Rolan."

The man grinned, showing a silver tooth, then drew a whip from his belt and strode forward with a swagger. Tom's heart thumped in his chest. His mind raced. *How has it come to this?* But as the brute before him cracked his whip, Tom's thoughts cleared. He sank into a crouch, sword raised.

The leather whip snapped towards

him. Tom sidestepped the blow and
angled his sword to catch the lash.
The leather wrapped about his blade.
Tom yanked his sword, tugging the
big man off balance, then thrust his
shield forward and up, driving it

hard into his opponent's jaw. *BOOF!*
The man fell back with a grunt,
dropping his whip, which unwound
from Tom's blade and hit the cobbles
with a clatter.

"You disobedient little wretch!"
Angelo shouted. Tom spun to find
the new king bearing down on him,
sword raised.

*I can't fight the king!* Tom lowered
his weapon and backed away, lifting
his shield in a gesture of surrender.
But Angelo strode on, teeth clenched
in a furious snarl, then lunged
and thrust. Tom blocked Angelo's
sword with the flat of his blade,
then staggered back, his whole arm
ringing with the impact. He gulped

as he started to circle the king, remembering the tales of Angelo's legendary strength. *I've never faced such a powerful swordsman. But I'm smaller and faster...*

Angelo thrust again, and Tom ducked sideways, then dived behind one of the carts, putting wood and baskets of grain between himself and the king's mighty sword arm.

"Please, sire," Tom said. "It wasn't my intention to show disrespect."

Angelo let out a low growl, then grabbed a handful of grain from a basket and flung it in Tom's face. As Tom put up a hand to shield his eyes, he felt his legs kicked out from under him. He landed on his back, winded, hearing his sword spinning away across the cobbles. He looked up through watering eyes to see Angelo glaring down at him.

"I'll teach you a lesson myself," snarled the king.

"STOP!" Hugo's voice rang out, loud in the morning air. Tom heard running, then a grunt and the scuffle of booted feet. He sat up, rubbing the chaff from his eyes, seeing Hugo wrestling to disarm his brother.

"Tom is our Master of the Beasts," Hugo said. "He is the most loyal subject I've ever known. I won't let you harm him."

"You've gone soft, Hugo," Angelo growled. "Why don't you just toddle off with your wife to Tangala, where cowards can prosper?"

"I'm no coward!" Hugo cried, still grappling with his brother's weapon. "I was as willing as you were to fight during the wars! It's not my fault Father sent you rather than me."

"No," Angelo hissed, "but once I went missing, you took my place quickly enough, didn't you?" Angelo lifted his voice, roaring right into Hugo's face, spittle flying. "You gave me up as dead and stole my throne!" Angelo thrust his brother away. Hugo staggered, then stood with his head down, his face flushing deep red.

"I was always ashamed for letting you perish in the North," Hugo said.

"If I had known you were alive…all this time…" His voice faltered.

Angelo let out a snort of disgust. "Save your pitiful excuses for someone who cares," he said. "Go to Tangala. I don't want to see you again." Then he turned back to Tom, still crouching on the cobbles, trying to catch his breath. "Now that Avantia has a strong ruler, capable of meeting any threat, it no longer needs a Master of the Beasts. Kapra!" Angelo called. Tom saw the witch standing in the shadow of the courtyard wall, smiling slyly. "Relieve the boy of all his powers and have him thrown in the dungeons."

Tom scrambled to his feet and

lunged for his sword, but before he could reach it, a sizzling, crackling blue light surrounded him. All his nerves seemed to catch fire at once. He fell to the ground, rigid and helpless, his muscles clenched with agony. Through the hideous pain, he felt a tug at his waist, and watched his jewelled belt unclasp itself and float away. The shield in his hand glowed, and as Tom watched, unable to move even a finger, each of the tokens flared a bright, lightning blue, then vanished. The strange light faded, and Tom slumped to the ground, every muscle spent. Huge hands gripped his shoulders and yanked him up, then hefted him into

the palace, along corridors and down
steps, through the shadowy passages
– and then, finally, into a cold stone
cell. As his captor released him, Tom
sank on to a dank cell floor, closed
his eyes and fell into darkness.

# 4

# TOM'S PUNISHMENT

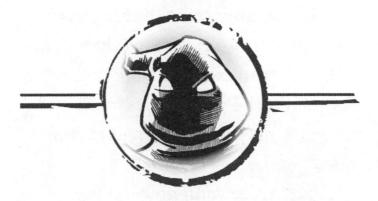

A loud squealing sound jolted Tom awake. He lifted his head and squinted into torchlight, seeing Captain Harkman stumble towards him. The heavy door was slammed shut behind the captain, leaving them in gloom.

"Are you all right?" Harkman asked.

"I think so." Tom tried shifting his

arms and legs as he sat up. It hurt, but they worked. "Are you?" He could just make out the captain's face in the thin grey light that filtered through a grate far above them. The old soldier looked too big for the tiny cell as he paced backward and forward, his hands chained before him.

"Apart from somehow having landed in a nightmare, I'm fine," Harkman said. "None of this makes sense! I know years of war can change a person, but Angelo is nothing like the brave young man I knew back when I was a boy. Something's wrong."

Tom cast his hazy memory back to

his fight with the dark-eyed king. He certainly seemed as strong as the legends told, and as good with a sword. Then, with a sudden jolt, Tom remembered something. "Was Angelo left-handed?" he asked Harkman.

"No," Harkman said, stopping abruptly. "Don't you remember the song? Angelo was famed for the legendary strength of his mighty *right* arm. And the Angelo I knew wouldn't team up with an evil witch, either. Like I said…something is very wrong. And I'll bet anything that it's Kapra's doing."

Tom felt a sudden rush of heat all over his body, then a tingling sensation that quickly died away, leaving him feeling colder and weaker than ever. *What was that?* He shook his aching head, trying to focus his mind. *It was probably just the shock*, he told himself.

"I suppose Angelo might have been wounded in battle, and lost full use of his right arm," Tom said. Before Captain Harkman could reply, heavy footsteps rang loudly in the passage outside.

"Please yourself," a harsh voice barked. The cell door swung open, and Aduro hobbled in carrying a torch, which he set in a sconce on the wall as the door banged shut behind him.

"What are you doing here?" Harkman asked, quietly, so as not to be overheard. "Not fallen foul of His Majesty as well, have you?"

"Not yet," Aduro whispered, lowering himself on to an upturned crate. "Angelo allowed me to come and visit you because I am *a foolish old man with no powers* – if I remember his words correctly. I thought you would benefit from something to eat." Aduro drew a loaf of bread wrapped in cloth from the folds of his cloak and set it down before him.

"We'd benefit more from knowing what in the world is going on!" Harkman said.

"You are not the only one," Aduro answered.

"Harkman thinks Angelo's

changed," Tom said. "And now he's fighting with his left hand. You knew him before he went to war, Aduro. Do you think he's different?"

"He has certainly gained a foul temper in his years away," Aduro said, frowning. "And his judgement seems to have suffered. But he spent many years in exile, locked in endless fighting…who knows what that would do to a person?"

"But what about this business with Kapra?" Captain Harkman said. "I can't believe she helped our troops win a battle, no matter what our new king says."

Aduro nodded thoughtfully, his face looking more lined than ever

in the deep shadows thrown by the torch. "It certainly seems strange," he admitted.

Frustration and anger welled up

inside Tom. "I have to escape," he hissed. "I need to find out what really happened—" The sound of yet more booted feet from outside the cell silenced him.

A moment later, the door burst open and a fair-haired, muscular soldier filled the opening, pointing at Tom.

"You! Out!" he snapped, jerking a thumb towards the passageway.

*About time!* Tom thought. *Maybe now I'll get some answers.* He leaped to his feet and hurried from the cell. Aduro joined them, but as Harkman followed, the big guard shoved him roughly back through the door and slammed it shut.

The brawny soldier marched away without a backward glance. Tom's mind raced as he and Aduro followed the guard along passageways and up flights of stairs. *I need to find Daltec. We have to come up with a plan...* Finally, the soldier thrust open the main palace doors, gesturing Tom through.

Rough hands grabbed Tom's shoulders as soon as he stepped into sunlight. He struggled, but a pair of armoured guards held him fast.

"Wait!" Aduro cried, but his words trailed off as the guards jerked Tom off his feet and hauled him into the courtyard where the feast had taken place the night before. Bunting still hung over the square, but apart from that, it couldn't look more different — the tables had been cleared away, and in the centre of the open space stood a hefty wooden chopping block. Sick dread washed over Tom. Beside the block stood a tall, hooded man, dressed all in black. A crowd had gathered, silent and watchful.

"Oof!" Reeling from a hefty shove to the back, Tom stumbled forward, landing on his knees before the chopping block. Up close, Tom could see score marks and dark staining on the wood. *Blood!* he thought, as rough hands pinned him down.

Suddenly, a hushed murmur ran through the crowd. Tom glanced

up as far as he could, seeing King Angelo sweep into the courtyard.

The king lifted a hand. "Today, we will see justice," Angelo shouted, his harsh voice echoing in the silence. "This boy is to be executed for disrespecting the crown. But first..." Angelo turned and gestured with an open palm to a pair of soldiers hefting between them a small black cauldron. They set it down in the centre of the square where Tom kneeled, some of the contents slopping over the edge. The liquid glinted in the sun, quickly hardening on the cobbles.

*Gold?* Tom stared at the shiny metal, frowning. Then suddenly, his whole body flushed hot, then cold. Panic squeezed his chest, snatching his breath away as a horrible realisation clamoured inside his skull. *No...no...it can't be...* But he remembered the strange tingling he'd felt in his cell the night before... the unshakable dread he felt now. Normally, his golden breastplate would give him the courage to face anything, but today, he felt only fear.

*Angelo has melted my Golden Armour!*

Trembling with rage and horror, Tom looked up to see the king striding towards him, his eyes flashing with cruel triumph.

"What were you thinking?" Tom cried, his voice ragged with emotion. "You've just destroyed an ancient artefact that has helped keep Avantia safe for centuries! Now, no

Master of the Beasts will ever wield that power again!"

Angelo leaned in so low that Tom could see the threads of red in the king's bloodshot eyes, and a thick vein throbbing at his temple. "Avantia needs no Master of the Beasts when its king is its finest warrior," Angelo said. "The armour serves no more purpose. And neither do you!" The king's voice dropped to a low growl only Tom could hear. "There's no Hugo to save you now!" Then he stood abruptly, and stepped away, lifting a hand as he nodded to the tall man in black.

As the hooded figure strode towards him, Tom glanced about

frantically, but couldn't see any of his friends among the silent, watching faces. *Elenna? Daltec? Aduro? Where are you? Someone has to help me!*

Tom's guard shoved his head suddenly downwards, so his cheek struck the wooden chopping block with a crack. The hooded man stepped back, raising an axe, which gleamed in the sunlight.

"Off with his head!" Angelo cried.

Muscles taut with fear, Tom closed his eyes and waited for death.

# INTO THE WILDLANDS

Sharp claws of terror scratched at Tom's heart as he waited for the axe to fall. *This has to be a nightmare.* But then he heard the axeman's leathers creak...the hiss of sharp metal slicing through air...

*THUNK!*

"AAAARGGH!" The cry came from

right above him. Tom opened his eyes to see the hooded man staggering back, dropping his axe. An arrow had pierced the flesh of his hand. At the rear of the crowd, Elenna was perched on a cart, lowering her bow.

*Thank you, my friend!* Tom leaped to his feet with a roar, wrenching himself from his captor's grip. Spinning round, he drove a knee into the soldier's gut.

"Seize him!" Angelo cried. Two soldiers bundled towards Tom, one from either side. Tom shot out his elbow, cracking one across the jaw. He swept the other's legs away with a low kick. Then he ran.

"Tom! To me!" Elenna cried, ready

to give him cover with her bow.

"Don't let him get away!" Angelo roared. Tom glanced back to see a group of soldiers eyeing Elenna anxiously, their swords half raised. He sped towards his friend, the crowd parting before him.

"This way!" Elenna hissed, leaping down from the cart as he reached her.

"This isn't the way to the gate!" Tom said.

"Trust me," Elenna answered, skirting around the palace walls, keeping low to stay hidden behind the gathered townsfolk. Finally, she reached an open space near the battlements. *A dead end!* Tom realised. But then he spotted Daltec waiting at the base of the wall, a bundle clutched in his arms.

He beckoned to them frantically. "Quick!"

"Out of the way!" an angry voice shouted. Yelps and screams broke out close behind them, along with the scuffle of feet.

The young wizard shoved the bundle into Tom's arms. Then he muttered a brief spell as he made a fist, casting a glowing blue orb towards the courtyard wall. The orb burst apart in a searing flash of light as it hit the stone, creating a circular portal. On the far side, rather than houses and streets, Tom could see

murky brown water overshadowed
by twisted mangrove trees. *A portal
to another realm!*

"Go!" Daltec said. "This portal
will take you to the Wildlands in the
north."

Tom hesitated, hearing the marching boots approach. "But what about you?" he asked.

"I'll stay here, hidden, to keep an eye on King Angelo." With another flash of searing light, Daltec vanished. Tom glanced back to see a troop of armoured guards pushing through what remained of the crowd.

"Hurry!" he told Elenna, then leaped through the portal. All the colours of the courtyard melded together, and the sound of the approaching soldiers cut off at once...

*SPLASH!* He landed ankle-deep in squelchy mud. A stench like rotten eggs hit him, and he blinked, his eyes adjusting to the sudden low light. A moment later, Elenna sploshed down beside him. A gentle *pop* made him glance back. The portal had gone. *Daltec saved us!* Tom sank to his knees in the gloom, suddenly weak with relief. Gnarled trees rose in a tangle of roots from waterlogged soil all around him. Their dark trunks crowded close together, meeting overhead to form a shadowy tunnel. Pools of stagnant water mirrored the dense canopy above, and narrow ridges of mud formed treacherous pathways through the swamp.

"Are you all right?" Elenna asked.

Tom looked down at the bundle in his arms to see his hands shaking violently. Visions flashed through his mind: the glinting axe, the bloody chopping block... Normally, he could call on the strength of heart that his magical chainmail gave him. *But now that Angelo's melted the armour, that magic is gone for ever...*

Tom heaved himself to his feet. "They were going to cut my head off," he gasped.

Elenna nodded. "That was way too close. But, thanks to Daltec, we're both still in one piece. What did he give you?"

Tom unwrapped the bundle,

drawing out his sword, then his
shield. It was little more than a
smooth plate of wood now, with
only slight indentations to show
that the magical tokens were
missing. He showed it to Elenna,

his shoulders sagging with defeat.
"We'll have no magic to help us on
this Quest at all," he said. The panic
he'd been fighting rushed back all
at once.

To Tom's surprise, Elenna

smiled gently, resting a hand on his shoulder. "Do you remember your first Quest, where you left Errinel with no weapons at all, not even your sword?" she asked. "Well, you didn't do too badly. And you've got something else now that you didn't have back then, too."

"What?" Tom asked.

"Experience!" Elenna said, then she punched his arm. "And me, of course!"

Tom found himself smiling too, the horror of what had just happened fading a little. With a nod, he sheathed his sword, then slung his shield on his back. "You're right," he said. "We can do this! I think we should look for some kind of town or settlement. The people here might know something about Angelo and his men."

Elenna nodded. She pointed along a bank of mud and scrappy sedge winding away through the swamp. "That way looks as good as any."

Tom and Elenna set off, picking their way between branching mangrove roots. The mud sucked at their boots with each step, sending up the clammy stench of rotting vegetation. Not so much as a frog or a bird chirped in the stillness. *It's too quiet...* Tom thought, the hairs on his scalp prickling as they trudged on through the gloom, keeping to the higher ground, sometimes leaping from one muddy island to the next. He squinted, looking for any sign of a village or camp nearby.

A faint *plop* sounded behind them. Tom whirled around to see circles rippling outwards across the surface of a silty pool. Nothing else moved.

After a few more steps, Tom heard a faint, rasping hiss, like scales sliding over wood. He turned, a tingle of fear tracing his spine. Still, he saw nothing.

"I can't help feeling something's following us," Tom said, his voice sounding too loud in his ears.

Elenna shivered, but she shook her head. "Surely we'd see broken branches, or some other sign…"

Gazing into the greenish-brown water ahead, Tom froze, heart thumping. Half buried in the murky darkness at the bottom of the swamp, he saw the pale, ghostly shapes of bones. He gripped Elenna's arm and pointed. A narrow ribcage poked up from the mud, connected to other bones including a long skull with sharp canines. Countless tiny skeletons surrounded it.

Tom quickly made out rodents, and birds, and an ox's horned skull. With a surge of horror, he spotted the dark eyes and gaping mouth of a half-mummified human skull.

Elenna hugged herself, staring

down at the watery graveyard. Then she took a deep breath. "I think you're right," she said, "something deadly must live here. And it has a good appetite too, by the looks of it." A twig cracked somewhere, and they both jumped.

"We need a better vantage point," Tom said, starting to clamber up the thickest trunk within reach, heading for the canopy above as Elenna shimmied up the broad trunk behind him. "If there's something coming, we should be able to see it from up here."

As Tom reached for the mangrove's high, curved branches, the tree shuddered so violently he lost his

grip. But before he could fall, the
branches around him sprang to life
like a nest of snakes, whipping and

writing, catching hold of his wrists. He gasped as another thick branch wrapped about his chest, crushing his ribs in a vice-like grip.

Beneath him, Elenna tugged at a wooden noose around her waist. "Get off me!" she cried.

*The tree's attacking us*, Tom realised.

# THE SWAMP MONSTER

Dangling in the clutches of the vast mangrove, Tom bucked and twisted, fighting to get free. But the branches holding him tightened, squeezing the breath from his chest. He heard Elenna let out a strangled cry.

"Don't fight them!" Tom gasped.

"They just get tighter!" As Elenna fell still, Tom felt a sickening lurch of movement. He looked down to see the tree's pale roots tugging themselves from the ground with squelching pops, groping over the mud, slapping and splashing through the shallow water. Then they started to slither over the ground like the many legs of an octopus.

*The tree can walk!*

It carried Tom and Elenna off the reedy bank, and into the dark waters of the skeleton graveyard. Then it stopped. With a sudden wrench, Tom felt himself tugged downwards, closer to the broad

trunk. Two knots in the wood
glowed like the red coals at the
heart of a fire. *Eyes?* Beneath them,

a wide crack opened, lined with jagged tooth-like spurs. *The tree is a Beast!* Tom realised. *And without my red jewel, I can't even reason with it!*

Noxious gas belched from the tree-Beast's maw as it widened, making Tom's eyes water. He spotted scraps of cloth and hunks of half-digested flesh snagged on teeth coated in a pale, oozing fluid. His stomach clenched with fear and horror. *It digests people in its trunk!*

Tom jerked his trapped sword arm downwards, trying to tug it free. But instead, he felt the tree's branches squeeze his wrists and chest even tighter. He gasped with agony. Above him, Elenna let out a whimper of pain.

*It's going to crush our bones to dust!* Tom forced himself to relax his body, going limp and heavy, like he'd passed out. When he felt the Beast's grip loosen a fraction, he took a deep breath and yanked his sword arm downwards once more, with as much strength as he could muster. The force scraped the skin from his wrist, but his hand came free! He snatched his sword from its sheath and hacked at the branch that was crushing his chest. As blade met wood, the tree-Beast gave a rasping screech, releasing its grip on Tom and letting him plummet to the ground. Elenna gave a yelp of surprise as she too fell.

*SPLASH!* Water and thick mud

closed over Tom's head as he landed on his back in the swamp. He tried to scramble up, and managed to get his head above water — but when he planted his feet, the soft mud shifted, and he started to sink.

Plastered with filth, Elenna broke the surface beside him, then gestured towards the nearest bank, on her right. "That way!" she cried.

But towering above them both was the Beast, its toothy maw spread into a wide, evil grin. A pale root flicked towards Tom. He sliced it off. Another tendril lashed at Elenna. Tom lopped it in half before it could reach her. With each strike, the tree-Beast let out a hideous

screech of rage. Branches lashed
through the air and roots whipped
out in a frenzy of fury. Tom chopped
and sliced, all the while trying to
edge sideways towards the bank
after Elenna. Soon, fragments of

pale root wriggled like maggots in the muddy water all around him.

His arm muscles burned with the effort, and his breath came in gasps. *I don't know how much longer I can keep this up!* He glanced towards Elenna to see her dragging herself up out of the water on to the reedy bank.

At the same moment, Tom felt a powerful grip close about his ankle, and pull…

Tom's stomach leaped into his mouth and everything spun as the branch yanked him off his feet and swung him upside down. All the blood rushed to his head. His sword slipped from his muddy grip and plunged into the swamp. A vile, squelching gurgle bubbled up from the Beast's throat. Its toothy jaws spread so wide that Tom could see luminous acid and half-digested bones churning deep inside its gut. A second branch clamped tightly around Tom's chest and thrust him headfirst towards the gaping maw.

Terror seared through him. *It's going to eat me alive!*

# 7

# THE HEART OF
# THE BEAST

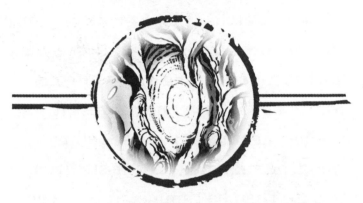

Tom gasped for breath, his eyes and
throat burning from the poisonous
gases pouring out of the Beast's
open mouth. Just a hand's breadth
from his face, strings of toxic drool
dripped from its needle-sharp teeth.
Tom thrust out his arms, gripping
the wood either side of the open

mouth, but he could feel his arms buckling, his hands slipping, as the Beast mercilessly pulled him closer.

"Tom! Catch!" Elenna called. Tom glanced over his shoulder to see her hurl something long and white his way. *A bone!* With one hand still wedged against the Beast's slimy wood, he snatched the missile from the air. Then he rammed it between the jaws, wedging them apart. The Beast's red eyes burned with fury. It let out a choking roar, blasting Tom with flecks of burning slime. Tom's head swam, and he felt searing points of pain on his arms and face where the acid blistered his flesh. The brittle bone bent and splintered

as the Beast tried to close its jaws.

*I have to get away!*

"Stay still, Tom!" Elenna called.
He heard a *whoosh*, then saw one
of Elenna's arrows slam deep into
the Beast's glowing eye. The branch

that held him suddenly went slack, and he tumbled headfirst into the swamp. Panic gripped him as his hands and knees sank deep and sludge filled his nostrils. Every movement seemed to work him further into the sucking, squelching bog.

His breath burning in his chest, Tom suddenly had an idea. *Instead of fighting the mud, I have to work with it!* With gentle, painfully slow movements, he started to ease his arms and legs forward as if swimming against a strong tide. The mud shifted around him, and he felt a flicker of hope. *Yes! It's working!* He kept going, hoping his breath would last, working himself slowly towards the surface. Just as he thought his throbbing lungs might burst, he thrust his head out into daylight and sucked in a huge gulp of air.

Tom started to pull himself free of the sucking swamp. But, with a whistling crack, a pale tree root coiled around his middle and yanked him up once more.

As the Beast lifted Tom clear of the mud, he caught sight of Elenna, glaring down an arrow, ready to shoot. A tree branch whipped out behind her, lashing at her temple. She slumped down among the reeds on the bank.

Tom managed to gasp a breath before the Beast plunged him down below the swamp's dark surface once more. Still dizzy and weak from lack of air, he opened his eyes to see a blur of bones spread in the

murk below him. He could feel the beat of his heart in his lungs. His whole body screamed for air. *This is it! After all my Quests, I'm going to die at the bottom of a swamp, the victim of a Beast whose name I*

*don't even know…*

Red dots swam at the edges of his vision, and an amber light seemed to throb before his eyes. His lungs shuddered. Suddenly, he realised the soft light wasn't his mind imagining something…it was real. He blinked, forcing his eyes to focus. At the bottom of the swamp, where the Beast's snaking roots mingled with mud and the bones of its prey, Tom could see a pulsating knot of amber wood.

The strange, rhythmic flaring of the light seemed like an echo of the pulse thudding in Tom's ears. Hope flooded through him. *That must be the Beast's heart! If I can just keep going a little longer, there may be a way to defeat this Beast after all!*

# THE LITTLE HERO

Tom pushed his pain and panic to the back of his mind. Then he kicked as hard as he could, dragging the tree root behind him, all his energy focused on the beating amber heart.

After what felt like an age, Tom reached the mud layer at the bottom of the swamp. The strange throbbing light, almost in reach now, glinted off something half buried in the silt nearby. *My sword!* Tom reached a hand into the sludge, groping clumsily for his weapon. Weak and half-blinded by lack of air, it took three tries to grasp the hilt.

He barely had anything left as he drew back his arm above the Beast's heart.

*If I'm going to die down here, I'll take the Beast with me...*

With the last remnants of his strength, he stabbed. To Tom's fading vision, it seemed as if the amber glow flickered, and went out. A distant part of him felt the root around his waist relax. But

Tom couldn't make his air-starved
arms and legs move. He sank slowly
through the water, soft blackness
surrounding him. Even the burning
need to breathe seemed far away.

He let his eyes fall shut...

A powerful grip closed about his

wrist, digging into the bone. He felt
a rushing, pulling sensation. *No! The
Beast is supposed to be dead!* Bright
light dazzled him as he was dragged
through slippery mud. He felt his
mouth wrenched open and his head
turned to the side, then a sudden
blow to his chest.

Burning water spewed from his
mouth. He coughed and gasped,
gratefully sucking in air. He looked
up to see Elenna peering anxiously
at him.

"You're alive!" she said.

"The Beast?" Tom croaked.

Elenna pointed to the blackened,
twisted remains of a tree standing
alone in the swamp. Its wizened

branches drooped lifelessly downwards, and a splintered gash replaced the gaping hole that only moments before had been the Beast's mouth. Tom's whole body sagged with relief. "Whatever you

were up to down below the water, it worked," Elenna said.

A chorus of loud hoots and gruff shouts started up from all around them. Elenna jumped to her feet, her bow raised. Tom struggled up beside her.

"We're surrounded!" Elenna hissed. Tom tightened his grip on his sword. At least twenty tall, muscular men and women with long braided hair had emerged from the mangrove trees, shouting and thumping their barrel chests.

Tom lifted his sword weakly, but realised how weak he and Elenna must look. Scrawny and tired, dripping with mud, a single sword and a bow against countless rusty knives and curved blades. *Still... while there's blood in my veins, I'll fight!* Tom thought. He clenched his jaw and stood taller.

A powerfully built, leathery-skinned man with grey hair and sharp blue eyes stepped forward and lifted his hand. The din of hooting and chest-thumping ceased at once.

"Greetings, young ones," the grey-haired man said, in the same strange accent as Angelo's head bodyguard. "Put down your weapons; we mean you no harm."

Tom and Elenna exchanged a frown, but kept their weapons

firmly raised.

"We did not intend to alarm you with our cheers," the old man went on. "We only mean to congratulate our little hero on his victory. We have been trying to kill the Beast,

Querzol, for years. My men are impressed that one so small can fight so bravely." The man spread his hands, showing clearly he held no weapon. "Why do you fear us?"

Tom gaped, unable to keep the

note of disbelief from his voice. "Because we are Avantians," he said. "Because our troops only just returned from defeating your barbarian army. We are at war!"

The old man's face creased into a bemused frown. "Barbarians?" he said. "We've not been called that for a good long while. We are the free folk now. The Avantian war ended many years ago. We have no reason to fight you again. We have troubles enough of our own."

Tom and Elenna shared another glance, this time wide-eyed and with eyebrows raised. They let their weapons fall to their sides. *Now we're starting to get answers*, Tom thought. *Angelo's been lying…*

"We heard different news in Avantia," Tom said. "But now it is clear we have been deceived. Can you tell us more about the war and how it ended?"

The grey-haired man shrugged, a smile spreading across his lined, weather-beaten face. "Of course," he said. "But we owe you more than just news. My name is Carwin. Come dry yourself at our fire and eat. We will celebrate the Beast's demise together, and I will tell you all that I know about the wars!"

Tom's stomach growled suddenly, and he realised all at once just how cold and hungry he felt. "Thank

you," he said, returning the man's warm smile. "Fire and food would be very welcome indeed."

*And it will also give us the perfect opportunity to find out what*

*Angelo's up to*, he thought, as he and Elenna followed the old man towards the fire.

"I think we've earned some dinner," Elenna joked.

Tom nodded, returning her smile. "But we mustn't stay too long. There are still three more Beasts out there…"

### THE END

# CONGRATULATIONS,
## YOU HAVE COMPLETED THIS QUEST!

At the end of each chapter you were awarded a special gold coin.
The QUEST in this book was worth an amazing 8 coins.

Look at the Beast Quest totem picture inside the back cover of this book to see how far you've come in your journey to become

MASTER OF THE BEASTS.

The more books you read, the more coins you will collect!

Do you want your own
Beast Quest Totem?

1. Cut out and collect the coin below
2. Go to the Beast Quest website
3. Download and print out your totem
4. Add your coin to the totem
www.beastquest.co.uk/totem

550+ COINS
# MASTER OF THE BEASTS

410 COINS
# HERO

350 COINS
# WARRIOR

230 COINS
# KNIGHT

180 COINS
# SQUIRE

44 COINS
# PAGE

8 COINS
# APPRENTICE

# READ ALL THE BOOKS IN SERIES 23:
## THE SHATTERED KINGDOM!

QUERZOL
THE SWAMP MONSTER

KROTAX
THE TUSKED DESTROYER

TORKA
THE SKY SNATCHER

XERKAN
THE SHAPE STEALER

*Meet three new heroes with the power to tame the Beasts!*

Amy, Charlie and Sam – three children from our world – are about to discover the powerful legacy that binds them together.

They are descendants of the *Guardians of Avantia*, an elite group of heroes trained by Tom himself.

Now the time has come for a new generation to unlock the power of the Beasts and fulfil their destiny.

*Read on for a sneak peek at how the Guardians first left Avantia by magic…*

Karita of Banquise gazed in awe at Tom, Avantia's mighty, bearded Master of the Beasts.

Under his leadership, she and her companions would today face their greatest challenge.

Tom pointed towards the brooding Gorgonian castle. "We must recover the chest of Beast Eggs Malvel stole," he reminded them. His fierce blue eyes moved from Karita to the others. Dell of Stonewin, whose bloodline connected him to Beasts of Fire; Fern of Errinel, linked to Storm Beasts; Gustus of Colton, bonded with Water Beasts.

"Malvel will be expecting an attack," Tom said. "His power is lessened, but he is still formidable." His eyes locked on Karita. "Stealth will be our greatest ally."

Karita felt as though her whole life had been a preparation for this moment. Countless hours spent studying the ancient tomes, day after day of gruelling combat training, months learning how to influence the will of Stealth Beasts and control the powers that filled the Arcane Band at her wrist.

But was she ready?

She gazed into Tom's face, and her doubts faded.

*Yes!*

A low rumble came from the

castle. Flashes of green lightning shot from the clouds as a swarm of screeching creatures erupted from the battlements.

Karita shuddered as Malvel's hideous minions streaked through the sky. They were man-sized, with white hides, limbs tipped with hooked claws and gaping jaws lined with sharp teeth. Their leathery wings cracked like whips.

"Karrakhs!" muttered Tom. "Karita – go!"

She nodded and slipped away behind jagged rocks. She turned to see the swarm of foul creatures engulf her companions. Tom's sword flashed. Howls rang out from the Karrakhs. The Guardians were using their Arcane Bands to form weapons that spun and slashed!

Karita raced for the castle, keeping low behind the ridge of rocks. Reaching the walls, she climbed up a gnarled vine and found a narrow window to crawl through. She looked back again. Tom and the Guardians had battled their way through the castle gates.

*Well fought!*

She dropped into a room and crept to the door. Torches burned in the corridor, casting shadows. The castle was silent, but Karita felt a growing dread as she slipped along the walls.

She knew where the chest of Beast eggs was hidden. But would Malvel allow her to get to them?

She came to a circular room, and saw the chest standing by the wall. Her heart hammering, Karita opened the lid and gazed down at the eggs. They were different sizes, shapes and colours. One slipped from the pile and she caught it in her gloved hand. It was pale blue, about the size of a goose egg. Acting on instinct, she slipped it inside her breastplate.

*Crash!*

She spun around. Malvel stood against the room's closed door.

"Did you really think you could enter my domain unseen?" he snarled, a green glow igniting in his palm. His voice was weaker than she'd imagined. "I *wanted* you to come here. After all, only a Guardian can hatch a Beast Egg."

Karita swallowed hard, seeking a way to escape.

"You and your friends will hatch these Beasts and I will drink in their power," growled the wizard. "I will become mighty again and Avantia will bow before me!"

"I'm not afraid of you!" Karita shouted.

A ball of green fire exploded from Malvel's hand. Karita dived aside, seared by the heat.

She leaped up, thrusting her right arm towards the wizard. The Arcane Band began to form a weapon, but another blast of fire sent her sliding across the floor.

Malvel loomed over her, both hands

burning green. Before he could strike, the door burst open and Tom and the Guardians rushed into the room.

"No!" roared Malvel. "Where arc my Karrakhs?"

"Defeated!" shouted Tom, whirling his sword to deflect Malvel's green flames. "Guardians! Take the eggs!"

Fern dived for the chest, but a blast from the wizard knocked her over.

"The eggs are mine!" howled Malvel. He traced a large circle of fire in the air. There was a blast of hot wind as the flaming hoop crackled and spat.

Malvel snatched up the chest and turned to the heart of the fiery circle.

"He's opened a portal!" shouted

Tom. "Stop him!"

Gustus ran at the wizard and wrested the chest from his grip. Roaring in anger, Malvel launched a fireball, but Fern managed to shove Gustus out of its path. But the force of her push knocked Gustus into the portal. With a stifled cry, he and the chest of eggs were gone.

"No!" Fern shouted, diving in after him. With a shout, Dell ran after her.

"Wait!" shouted Tom.

"It's our duty to protect the eggs!" Dell called back as he disappeared into the swirling portal.

Malvel sprang forward, but Tom bounded in front of him, holding him back with his spinning blade as the wizard hurled magical fireballs.

Karita saw the walls of the portal writhing and distorting. Malvel's fireballs were making it unstable. At any moment it might vanish!

Tom was knocked back by a torrent of green fire as the wizard turned and leaped into the portal. Karita flung herself after him.

"No! Karita!" The last thing she heard was Tom's voice. "The portal is in flux! You could be sent anywhere!"

And then there was nothing but a rushing wind and howling darkness, as she plunged into the unknown.

*Look out for*
*Beast Quest: New Blood*
*to find out what happens next!*